JUV/E8
FIC
BERNSTEI

EASTSI

Chicago Public Library

W9-BBP-794

RO405021552

My brother, the pest

DISCARD

CHICAGO PUBLIC LIBRARY
VODAK EASTSIDE BRANCH
3710 EAST 106 STREET
CHICAGO, IL 60617

A Note to Parents

Welcome to REAL KIDS READERS, a series of phonics-based books for children who are beginning to read. In the classroom, educators use phonics to teach children how to sound out unfamiliar words, providing a firm foundation for reading skills. At home, you can use REAL KIDS READERS to reinforce and build on that foundation, because the books follow the same basic phonic guidelines that children learn in school.

Of course the best way to help your child become a good reader is to make the experience fun—and REAL KIDS READERS do that, too. With their realistic story lines and lively characters, the books engage children's imaginations. With their clean design and sparkling photographs, they provide picture clues that help new readers decipher the text. The combination is sure to entertain young children and make them truly want to read.

REAL KIDS READERS have been developed at three distinct levels to make it easy for children to read at their own pace.

- LEVEL 1 is for children who are just beginning to read.
- LEVEL 2 is for children who can read with help.
- LEVEL 3 is for children who can read on their own.

A controlled vocabulary provides the framework at each level. Repetition, rhyme, and humor help increase word skills. Because children can understand the words and follow the stories, they quickly develop confidence. They go back to each book again and again, increasing their proficiency and sense of accomplishment, until they're ready to move on to the next level. The result is a rich and rewarding experience that will help them develop a lifelong love of reading.

To Michal, the big sister: You gave me the ideas
for this story. And to Naomi: Without you there
would be no story at all.
—M. B.

Produced by DWAI / Seventeenth Street Productions, Inc.
Reading Specialist: Virginia Grant Clammer

Copyright © 1999 by The Millbrook Press, Inc. All rights reserved. Published by
The Millbrook Press, Inc. Printed in the United States of America.

Real Kids Readers and the Real Kids Readers logo are trademarks of The Millbrook Press, Inc.

Library of Congress Cataloging-in-Publication Data

Bernstein, Margery.
   My brother, the pest / Margery Bernstein ; photographs by Dorothy Handelman.
        p.   cm. — (Real kids readers. Level 2)
   Summary: A girl has a terrible time getting along with her little brother, who is a pest, but
she comes to appreciate him when she needs a playmate to keep her company.
   ISBN 0-7613-2055-5 (lib. bdg.). —ISBN 0-7613-2080-6 (pbk.)
   [1. Siblings—Fiction. 2. Play—Fiction. 3. Stories in rhyme.] I. Handelman, Dorothy, ill.
II. Title. III. Series.
PZ8.3.B45854My   1999
[E]—dc21   98-35822
                                                                        CIP
                                                                        AC

pbk: 10 9 8 7 6 5 4 3 2 1
lib: 10 9 8 7 6 5 4 3

EAS

My Brother, the Pest

By Margery Bernstein
Photographs by Dorothy Handelman

The Millbrook Press
Brookfield, Connecticut

Chicago Public Library
Vode??? ???de Branch
3710 E. ???th St.
Chicago, IL 60617

I had a big fight
with my brother, the pest.
He makes me so mad!
Let me tell you the rest.

R0405029532

My life was just fine
till *that kid* came.
But here's what he did.
He messed up my game.

He took my best markers.
He took them all.
He drew in my book.
He drew on my wall!

If *I* did that,
Mom would say it was bad.
I'd get a time-out,
and Dad would be mad.

But *he* has it easy
because he is small.
Mom only told him,
"Don't draw on the wall."

That pest always copies
the things that I do.
If *I* have some milk,
then *he* wants some too.

If *I* wear a red shirt
when I go to bed,
then *he* wants one too.
"Red!" he yells. "Red!"

That kid is a brat.
It's really not fair.
He doesn't take turns,
and he doesn't share.

He sits on Mom's lap,
and that is just fine.
But when *I* want a turn,
"No!" he yells. "Mine!"

If we get a treat
from a store in the mall,
I don't mind sharing.
But *he* wants it all.

He gives me a pain.
He bugs me a lot.
He thinks he is cute.
I think he is not.

What can I do now?
I still want to play.
But he messed up my game,
so I put it away.

I could call a friend,
but Dad's on the phone.
It's no fun to play
when you're all alone.

Oh, no! It's the pest!
Who asked *him* in here?
I want him to go.
I don't want him near.

I know what *he* wants.
It's easy to see.
He brings in his books
and gives them to me.

I say, "Go away!"
I give him a look.
But he does not go.
He hands me a book.

SNAPPY Little NUMBERS

I give a big groan.
We sit on the floor.
I read him the book.
"More!" he says. "More!"

I read him more books,
and then we play school.
I am the teacher.
Hey! This is cool!

ALPHABET

Aa Bb Cc Dd Ee
Ff Gg Hh Ii Jj Kk
Ll Mm Nn Oo Pp
Qq Rr Ss Tt Uu Vv
Ww Xx Yy Zz

BALL

Art

"Come on," I tell him.
"Let's play a new game.
Just watch what I do.
Then you do the same."

He does what I do.
We have lots of fun.
We hop and we skip.
We jump and we run.

I *think* it's okay
if he copies me now.
I *think* he'll take turns
if I show him how.

I *think* I'd miss him
if he went away.
I'm glad that he's here
when I want to play.

You know, that kid
is really not bad.
He loves me a lot,
and that makes me glad.

Sometimes he's a pest.
Sometimes he's okay.
He's always my brother.
I guess he can stay.

31

Phonic Guidelines

Use the following guidelines to help your child read the words in *My Brother, the Pest*.

Short Vowels

When two consonants surround a vowel, the sound of the vowel is usually short. This means you pronounce *a* as in apple, *e* as in egg, *i* as in igloo, *o* as in octopus, and *u* as in umbrella. Short-vowel words in this story include: *bad, bed, big, bugs, but, can, Dad, did, fun, get, had, has, him, his, hop, kid, lap, let, lot, mad, Mom, not, red, run, sit.*

Short-Vowel Words with Consonant Blends

When two or more different consonants are side by side, they usually blend to make a combined sound. In this story, short-vowel words with consonant blends include: *asked, best, brat, brings, glad, hands, jump, just, milk, pest, rest, skip, went.*

Double Consonants

When two identical consonants appear side by side, one of them is silent. In this story, double-consonants appear in the short-vowel words *messed, miss, still, tell, till, yells,* and in the *all*-family, the words *all, call, mall, small, wall.*

R-Controlled Vowels

When a vowel is followed by the letter *r*, its sound is changed by the *r*. In this story, words with *r*-controlled vowels include: *more, shirt, store, turn.*

Long Vowel and Silent E

If a word has a vowel and ends with an *e*, usually the vowel is long and the *e* is silent. Long vowels are pronounced the same way as their alphabet names. In this story, words with a long vowel and silent *e* include: *came, cute, fine, game, life, makes, mine, same, take, time.*

Double Vowels

When two vowels are side by side, usually the first vowel is long and the second vowel is silent. Double-vowel words in this story include: *groan, pain, play, say, stay, treat.*

Diphthongs

Sometimes when two vowels (or a vowel and a consonant) are side by side, they combine to make a diphthong—a sound that is different from long or short vowel sounds. Diphthongs are: *au/aw, ew, oi/oy, ou/ow.* In this story, words with diphthongs include: *drew, how, new, now.*

Consonant Digraphs

Sometimes when two different consonants are side by side, they make a digraph that represents a single new sound. Consonant digraphs are: *ch, sh, th, wh.* In this story, words with digraphs include: *that, them, then, things, think, what, when, with.*

Silent Consonants

Sometimes when two different consonants appear side by side, one of them is silent. In this story, a word with a silent consonant is *know.*

Sight Words

Sight words are those words that a reader must learn to recognize immediately—by sight—instead of by sounding them out. They occur with high frequency in easy texts. Sight words not included in the above categories are: *a, am, and, away, be, because, come, could, do, does, from, gives, go, have, he, here, I, if, in, it, look, me, my, no, of, on, one, only, out, put, says, see, so, some, the, to, too, up, want, was, we, would, you.*